We Dissolve

Post-Progressive Fictions

Stephen V. Ramey

WE DISSOLVE: POST-PROGRESSIVE FICTIONS

Pokeberry books may be purchased for book club, educational, business, and promotional use. For information, email editor@ pokeberryexchange.com with your request.

ISBN 978-0-9972276-5-9
FIRST EDITION

Printed in the United States of America
Book Design by Stephen V. Ramey
Cover Design by Stephen V. Ramey
Photo Credit: Sharlene Reagan

Contents

To my wife, Susan Urbanek Linville, who keeps me on the up and up, and my daughter, Brittany, who reminds me to trim my beard. Without them, I would be an animal.

Also, a shout out to my brother, Ray, who so kindly posed for this cover. I may disagree with you from time to time, Bro, but that has never stopped me from respecting what you accomplish.

Foreward

It's been my observation that there are two basic mindsets. The Conservative aspires to a past that never was. The Progressive aspires to a future that will probably never be. Those of you who know me know that I have always belonged to the latter camp. Which makes it difficult to deal with the current political and social climate here in the United States of Merika.

Forty years of dumbing-down and dividing us has borne fruit. Facts are now futile, deep thoughts come gurgling up from the gut, confirmation bias too often rules both sides of the divide.

As Ayn Rand famously said:

> "You can avoid reality, but you cannot avoid the consequences of avoiding reality."

I'm not blind to the idea that a better tomorrow may grow from the desiccated dirt of these last few generations, but the point of this collection is that right here, right now, I am feeling a touch of the class division blues.

You hold in your hands my requiem for inclusion, equality, trust. There is a darkness to these tales, sprawling splashes of un-hope. Even so, there *is* hope and purpose for our endeavor.

Let us recall what the great Ernest Hemingway wrote:

> The world breaks everyone, and afterward, some are strong at the broken places.

The Life of Gum

We begin as bricks of chicle dumped into a hopper to be molded into a likeness wrapped in foil and sent into the world to bring flavor to some greater being's mouth, to be spat out when they are done and make our way—in that laboriously indirect way that is our life—into grainy loam fed upon by saplings. From the tree, to the tree, as the saying goes.

ORIGINALLY APPEARED IN *CRACK THE SPINE*

1

American Spirit Lights

Sylvie was six when she started smoking *American Spirit Lights*. It cut the bitterness of long afternoons cleaning other people's toilets and making their beds. The drawback, of course, was that she often had the jitters the next morning at kindergarten. It was *No Smoking* there or learn the error of your ways at the back of Mrs. Shepherd's hand. She never left marks, but she left plenty of scars.

This was Sylvie's second year in kindergarten, and she felt awkward among the smaller kids playing blocks or practicing their motor skills with construction paper and blunted scissors. Sylvie had little patience for blocks. Usually when playtime came she would stand off in the corner and watch, fingers veed to accommodate an imaginary cigarette. Imagination was the key to a happy life, her mother said. "You have to imagine those aches in your back are not real, imagine that your knee cap is supposed to move like that, imagine the lady you work for actually gives a fuck whether or not you are deported."

Of course, there was no danger of Sylvie being deported since she was born in this country, but she understood Mama's point. You had to imagine other people cared about you the way you cared about yourself. Otherwise, what was the point of dragging yourself out of bed each morning, walking to kindergarten, putting up with Mrs. Shepherd, doing an eight-hour shift of housework, just to come home to zap a burrito and go to bed? You had to imagine all that effort mattered, that it would carry you somewhere in the end. Some days it was hard. Some days she even had to imagine Mama's love. Mama never came home before ten, and sometimes she would bring a man. The grunting and sloppy laughter would keep Sylvie up all night and make the next day even worse. She smoked a full pack of *American Spirit Lights* on those days, and it cut into the money she could put toward their rent.

Lately, Mama had been seeing a bricklayer from the barrio, a man with one good eye who yelled and slapped when Sylvie was slow to bring his beer. Sylvie couldn't wait for this one to go away.

When she arrived home one day to find the apartment bricked in—bricks in the windows, a brick wall blocking the door—she imagined Mama was in there, happy at last in the castle she had built with her own industrious hands. This was what it was all for, this time of construction at the end of endless days of labor. A part of Sylvie wished her mother had waited until she got home to build her walls but wishing was not useful. Wishing was like stabbing a classmate with blunted scissors. It might leave a mark but wouldn't penetrate reality.

And so, Sylvie sat on urine-stained carpet in the hallway and scrounged through her purse for the last pack of *American Spirit Lights*. She tapped the final cigarette from its dented maw and lit it with a trembling hand. The first puff calmed her jitters. The second, she drew deep into her lungs, and held it there while daylight slipped slowly away from the pane at the hallway's end. It came to her that even though there was a brick wall between her and her mother, there was really nothing separating them at all.

ORIGINALLY APPEARED IN *THE DR. T.J. ECKLEBURG REVIEW*

Sugar-Coated Hairpin Curve

He-Man in the driver's seat, She-Man by his side. The top is down, the wind a hurricane in their ears. In the back, Baby-Man drowses between liquid-sweet life and taffy-sweet dream. The car is a candy red 1969 Camaro, tires underinflated to cope with the crackle-crazed topping of this winding black road down into the valley.

The pedal on the right is pushed. Hard. Asphalt sprays up from the sudden spin, a scent like burning licorice, lava lust, vodka in their morning mouths.

"Too fast," She-Man proclaims from the watcher's seat.

"Not fast enough," He-Man yells. "We're going to be late." For what? For life in the valley, of course.

The car hits a hairpin curve, slews left, slews right. Rubber stretches, bites, skids. A guardrail crunches, and suddenly they are flying, the granular city melting before them like a sugar glaze. Windows wink, flat-roofed buildings stare.

In the back seat, Baby-Man giggles deep down in his chest. His naked head comes wobbling up. And for just that instant all is right in his sugar-coated world.

ORIGINALLY APPEARED IN GARDEN GNOME

Infested

Our paranoia is infinite today. And not without reason. We have just endured a journey to and from Mars orbit in full view of the world. Areas of the ship that were supposed to be off limits were not. Every bowel movement, every wet dream and dry heave, a veritable sampler of trysts—it has all been broadcast, sprinkled across the globe like so much Hollywood glitter. The ultimate Reality Show, with our crew of six as unaware actors.

Jimmy found the first pinhole camera. He brought it to me, pinched between his fingers like an insect with overlong legs. A frown fixed on his blocky face. His blue eyes blinked and blinked again.

"Do you think there're others, Cap?"

Cockroaches came to mind.

"I doubt it," I said. "It's probably just a prototype. Where'd you find it?"

"In the toilet, next to the lid hinge, you know?"

I nodded. Inside I was cringing. If the company had sold access to "special" interest groups, they'd sold it to everyone. I could not prevent my eyes from tracking to the cabin wall. Any of those thousand rivets might be a camera.

"Back to your station," I told Jimmy.

"Should I look for more, Cap? Should I tell the others?"

"No," I said. "Let's keep this to ourselves for now, okay?"

"Sure, Cap." Jimmy turned crisply and left. The camera lay on my workstation, aimed at the far wall. With a shudder, I crushed it beneath a magnetic paperweight. One down, a thousand to go?

Of course I contacted Control.

"Really?" the tech said. I didn't recognize him. There's a lot of turnover in the control room.

"Really," I said, holding up the decapitated device.

The tech squinted. He frowned.

"Patch me through to Anderson," I said.

Liv Anderson didn't squint. She knew. I could see it in her steady gaze.

"You can be sure we'll get to the bottom of this, Captain Blevin," she said.

I can tell you the bottom of it, I thought. *The bottom line.*

Sharon came a few hours later. A tentative tap at the hatch, and I looked up to see her standing there, arms pressed tightly across her chest. She looked frantic, eyes darting from place to place, on the verge of tears.

"I found a camera in the crew quarters," she said. "In the shared laptop."

"How did you find it?" I said.

"The screen shorted, so I took it apart and... and..."

I stood. "It's okay."

She shook her head violently. "What if there are cameras here too? What if Carl sees... sees me... us?"

"It's okay," I said. *It's too late,* I thought. We were all married with kids, solid conservative family types in keeping with the current political climate. Month long isolation will do strange things to a psyche though. I don't care who you are.

"What will happen to us?" she said. "You'll lose your commission. I'll... I'll..."

"Let it go," I said. "We can't control how others react."

"No," she said, suddenly angry. "But we damned sure could have controlled our own behavior. How can you be so calm about this? Did you know?"

"Of course not," I said. "I would never do that to you."

She looked doubtful but turned and left the cabin without further comment.

By the next shift, the entire crew was in on the secret. They tore apart the sleeping room, inspected computers and lights and speakers, scratched paint from any protrusion or intrusion in the cabin walls.

Camera after camera found its way to my cabin, accompanied by infinitesimal microphones, sound amplifiers, night vision LEDs, you name it. I gave up trying to destroy them all.

Control continued to stonewall even with this pile of evidence. One bug, two maybe, but no way could they have launched a vessel infested with spying devices and not know about them. I told them to demand an updated schematic from the prime contractor, giving them a way out of the mess. They didn't bite. I used to envy Liv's composure. I grew to hate it now.

Yesterday, Gary found a bug in the main control panel, a listening device. He had to reroute a secondary thruster to get it out. Then Jimmy spotted a camera embedded in the airlock seal. By this time, the crew was frothing over this violation. I didn't point out that we'd signed waivers giving up many of our privacy rights. Standard protocol.

To date I had avoided searching my own cabin, but as the hours to re-entry counted down, I lost it. We were supposed to be heroes, not fodder for late night streaming. Every time I tried to work, I felt eyes staring at me through the screen. Every time I heard a voice, it came from outside the hull, a steady patter of gossip I could not quite make out.

When Jimmy appeared in my hatchway, I was elbow-deep in light panel circuitry.

"Cap?" he said. "Re-entry in forty minutes." His gaze took in the shrapnel I had harvested. "Ship intercom's out," he added. Then he turned to go, no explanation required.

Now, I'm strapped into the re-entry capsule, staring at a blank space where the cockpit viewport used to be. Buttons hang from wires. My fists clench the RCS control wheel as usual, but I have no idea whether the thrusters will continue to respond.

Gary sits in the copilot seat. He's long and lanky and usually gregarious. Now he's quiet, lips compressed behind the smoky face shield of his EVA suit. My own face shield is cracked. I shouldn't have done that, but it was staring at me.

"In ten, nine, eight," Gary says.

I feel the first lick of atmosphere, the slightest shudder. Already the cabin seems too hot.

"Here goes nothing," Jimmy says from behind us.

I almost hope we missed a camera. If the world is going to kill us, I'd like to make it watch.

ORIGINALLY APPEARED IN *DAILY SCIENCE FICTION*

Work Ethic

Manuel rolled the mop bucket to the next office, careful not to slosh soapy water. With two entire floors to clean by midnight, he had no time for sloppiness.

Mister Scott was working late, as usual. Tonight, he had someone in the office, a young man in an expensive suit like his.

Manuel tapped on the door frame. "Should I come back?"

Scott glanced over. A smile split his tanned face. "No, Manuel. Go ahead. I won't hold you up."

"Thank you, sir." Manuel guided the square yellow bucket into Mr. Scott's office, and pulled the dust cloth from his back pocket.

"I'm sorry," Scott said to the other man. "What can I tell you? The numbers just aren't there. In lean times, you have to buckle down and work harder."

"But we have a new baby," the man said, spreading his hands.

"Your wife has a new baby," Scott said. "You have a job."

"I can't believe you said that."

"I didn't," Scott said. "Just be sure that you heard it. If you want to remain with this firm, you've got to get those sales numbers up, even if it takes eighty-hour weeks, twenty hour days. That's called the American Dream. Right, Manuel?"

"*Si*, Sir."

"How many jobs to you have, Manuel?"

"Three. I will go from here to the WalMart at midnight." Manuel swiped the rag across filing cabinets. Clean from the top down, was his mantra.

"And how many children?" Scott said.

"Six."

The young man flinched. "But it's not the same, Mr. Scott." He looked morose. "This weekend's our anniversary. Things are touchy right now with Sandra."

"Success comes from hard work," Scott said. "There's no substitute."

"Yes, sir, I'll do better." The young man stood.

"I'll be watching," Scott said. "I expect to see your car when I arrive in the morning and see it again when I leave at night."

The young man left. Scott yawned and packed up his briefcase. Manuel slapped the wet mop onto the floor.

"Will you lock the door when you leave?" Scott said.

"Of course, Mr. Scott."

"Thank you, Manuel." He smiled encouragingly. "I wish we had a hundred employees like you."

Manuel swabbed in broad strokes until he no longer heard Mr. Scott's footsteps. He wrung the mop and swabbed again.

ORIGINALLY APPEARED IN *FIRST STOP FICTION*

The Valley of Doom

The light was failing as we started down Route 424 into the Valley of Doom. That wasn't its map name, but Bruce and I had called it that on our annual excursion over the mountains to Grandmother's house. Now it was my fiancé in the car with me, drowsing against the passenger window.

"Sasha," I said, "we're about to enter the valley. You might want to wake yourself up a bit so as to appreciate the splendor of our descent."

She yawned and sat straight. "It's quite... haunting," she said in that noncommittal tone of hers. I couldn't tell if she was serious.

"It's actually called Copper Wash Canyon," I said. "There's a river at the bottom, more like a creek, actually. I guess they had a copper mine down there at one time."

"The road winds down into the canyon like a ribbon turned back upon itself," Sasha said.

I gazed through the windshield. Sasha was right about the road, but she was also wrong. It did superficially resemble a ribbon, but it looked more like a stream of molten slag to me, white-hot liquid clotted with shadow, coiling down into darkness. I imagined a waterfall of sparks at its terminus, twisted men with goat horns pounding anvils, turning that light into the darker foundation of our world.

A sunset trick. The pavement would be gray, not white, and it could hardly flow. That was a river's business, not a road's, though I did recall reading that glass flows. Very slowly, the silicon pane distorts downward as its molecular structure gives in to gravity.

"How much farther?" Sasha said. Another yawn. A blink of those pretty eyes.

"From the valley opening it's maybe fifty miles through farmland." *As the corncob flies*, my dad used to say. He'd not been a fan of moving back to be with Mom's mom in her final years, but he had done it. That was the way a relationship should work, I supposed, but I always wondered. I hadn't been happy to leave middle school friends behind and take up high school on foreign terrain. Farm boys and apple pie girls, 4H and county fairs. The experience had marked me for sure.

"Do you think we could stop at a gas station?" Sasha said. "I need to pee."

"Sure, if we find one. It gets pretty desolate out here."

We drove through shadow and emerged to a new reality. The slope steepened. The road seemed to narrow. There was barely a berm now, just a metal guardrail like some lonely sentinel at the edge of oblivion. I clutched the steering wheel.

"Don't you think you should slow down?" Sasha said. She leaned away from the window. A hundred yards below, the road continued its molten descent.

We're part of the flow. It was a startling realization. The valley had us. The Valley of Doom.

I tapped the brake. The car slowed, but also pulled toward the guard rail.

Sasha smiled nervously. Her teeth were very white. "Do you think she'll like me?"

"Who, Mom?"

"Yes."

"Of course she'll like you. You're going to be her daughter." A tire hit something. The steering wheel twisted against my grip. Only momentarily, but it sent my heart pounding.

"I hope she likes me," Sasha said. "I'm sorry about your dad."

My inner child cringed. I thought of Dad lying in blood, the shotgun angled from his corpse like an unwilling accomplice. I'd only seen the one picture. They wanted me to understand Mom's mental state. They wanted to change my condemnation into comfort. And I had tried, I'd tried to put myself into her place and feel the agony (guilt?) that drove her into solitude. Mostly I pretended. Some emotions are impossible to steer.

It had been Sasha who insisted we visit before the wedding, Sasha who pushed me to re-approach my roots. And now, here we were, halfway down the valley, half-swallowed, half-lost. We were slag in the downhill flow.

How long before Sasha asked me to alter my dreams? How long until I gave up like Father? I wanted to design games. I wanted to write new worlds, create new paths for people to escape their mundane. I wanted—

Sasha placed her hand on my thigh. "Can we visit the cemetery?"

A shudder ran through me. "She had him... he was cremated."

"Did she keep the ashes?"

"I don't know."

"How could you...?" Her hand returned to her lap. "Should I call her Marion? Mrs. Stekolfsky? What do you think she'll want?"

"Marion, I think."

"Okay." Sasha peered through the side window. An eighteen-wheeler whooshed past. The car buffeted. I tapped the brake. The car pulled. I released. Our headlights illuminated only a few yards of the road ahead.

"I've been thinking," Sasha said. "What would you think about moving out here?"

"Here?"

"The job market is bad in the city," Sasha said. "It's not like either of us has great prospects."

"You'd rather farm?"

"No. Think of the cost of living, though. We could live on almost nothing. Maybe your Mom would take us in. I mean we could pay rent, but..."

"You don't even know if you'll like her," I said.

Sasha laughed lightly. "We can always leave. The road runs both ways."

Does it? I pressed the brake pedal. The car pulled toward the guardrail. I turned through the final curve into shadow.

ORIGINALLY APPEARED IN *STORY SHACK*

Reality TV

Click. Dancers leap through Global Warming. Male? Female? Human?

Click. "Unfuck the world!" Anonymous.

Click. A child. The toy in his hand reminds me of the remote in mine.

Click. Smoldering passion, man on man, race on race. Love?

Click. Lipstick belly, a smirk, a smile. Demarcation.

Click. Ourselves reflected. Suzie owl, me fox. Wise, sly, the perfect pair.

"You want to—"

"—order pizza?"

"You read my—"

"Mind?"

"Not a bit."

"Sausage?"

"Mushroom."

"We're dying."

"Doomed."

Her hand on mine, finger probing.

Click, click, click. We flip through time in snapshots, slapshots, a quantum need for change.

The Vain King

Once upon a time there was an extremely vain king who sired two sons and a daughter. Because of his indifference to anyone but himself, the sons constantly vied for his attention, fomenting one ill-conceived industry after another until the accumulation of their indiscretions became too weighty for even the king to ignore.

"This must stop," he proclaimed. "The time has come for me to choose one of you as my heir."

"But Father," the sons protested, "it is not your wealth we seek, but your respect."

"Enough," the king said. "I have made up my mind. All that remains is to determine the mechanism of my decision. It must be a process worthy of my legendary station."

"I have a thought," the daughter said. She had taken a different tack than her brothers, foregoing the example of their ostentatious public proclamations and public failures to learn her craft in the back alleys that any city possesses. Through a series of clandestine apprenticeships, she had amassed an arsenal of potions and poisons that rivaled any in the kingdom.

Witchcraft being illegal—the king had prohibited *any* activity that might empower women against him—the daughter had disguised her undertakings beneath a veneer of innovation, even inventing a syringe through which she might deliver her formularies. No 'Double double, toil and trouble' for her, but a simple, efficient needle prick. In fact, it was her nightly injections that kept the king vital beyond his years. His enemies might be legion, but none could outwork him.

And so it was that when the daughter spoke he did not dismiss or bully her, but leaned back and listened, mouth rounding with anticipation.

"A boxing match," she said. "Two princes, one ring, the future at stake."

"Barbarous," the elder son spat. "Bludgeoning each other like common street fighters hardly befits our station."

"It's called pugilism," the daughter corrected.

The king's hands spread—"Tremendous!"—retracted—"Fantastic"—and spread again—"Think of the ratings."

The daughter bowed to hide her secret smile.

The day of the event found the King and his daughter seated in a private balcony above a grandstand filled with chatting nobles. The remainder of the courtyard hosted temporary bleachers filled with stoic subjects. A tent marked either end of the platform where the contestants readied themselves.

The king beamed. "This is the largest audience ever to assemble." He leaned forward, hands clasped between his knees. "Not even my predecessor could draw this crowd."

The daughter stood. "Please excuse me, Father. I want to wish the princes good fortune."

"Prince," the king corrected. "One prince. One loser."

"Of course," the daughter said, and she hurried off clutching a sachet containing two syringes.

She visited the elder brother first. He was tall and elegant and not quite as gullible as the other.

"I brought you something," she said. She retrieved a syringe.

The brother frowned. "Is this what you inject into Father?"

"Similar," she said.

He considered. "It does help his stamina."

17

"And strength," the daughter said. She angled the syringe upward and pushed a drop from its tip.

The brother began to offer his arm but drew back. "No. I am taller. I have longer reach. The trainer tells me it is a simple matter of frustrating my opponent with the jab." He threw his fist forward a few times. "Finishing with an uppercut." He swung his arm up with such force the resulting breeze ruffled the daughter's dress.

"That *is* impressive," she said. "If you are certain you do not need this—" she jiggled the syringe "—I will offer it to our brother."

"Why?"

"I labored to distill this substance and do not wish to see it wasted."

The brother sighed. "Very well." He twisted his shoulder toward her. A jab, a grunt, and it was done.

The younger brother was even less eager. "What do I need of your potions?" he said. "I have been working out." He flexed his biceps. "One punch will crush him."

"I'm surprised to hear you say that," the daughter said. "Your brother *demanded* I give him an injection."

"He did?" He flexed his arm and closed his eyes.

By the time the princess returned to her seat, the two had touched gloves and stepped back. A cowbell clanked, and they came together.

The elder brother landed a jab that snapped the other's head back, then an uppercut that staggered him. The audience gasped, but the younger recovered. He charged, heedless of his foe's longer reach, to deliver a series of body blows that resounded through the gallery.

The elder brother toppled sideways clutching his chest.

"One," the referee shouted. "Two… Three…"

Also clutching his chest, the younger brother dropped to his knees, then onto his face. The two lay motionless as the referee finished his count.

Later, as the daughter prepared the king's injection, she said, "It's a shame they died. At least you have me."

"You?" The king's brow furrowed. "You are not a son."

"I have done more to support you than either of those useless men. I coaxed enemies to the negotiating table, cut your critics' quills. I even invented a *science* for you."

The king nodded absently. "There *is* a way that you might provide me an heir. These injections have left me as virile as ever."

The daughter paused, needle denting her father's skin. She pulled it back. "I forgot an ingredient." She dashed to her apothecary and back, hoping the king would not notice that the potion had changed color. But when had he ever noticed anything important?

"Ready?" she said. She pressed the syringe to his arm.

The king glanced away. "Tonight, you will come into my bed," he said as his daughter jabbed the needle in and pushed the plunger down.

The Naked Truth

He stands naked on the boardroom table, shriveled penis nested in the bowl of his sagging balls. The media thinks he's a freak, but what do we know about such things? He's the old man, the CEO, the guy who took us from a single retail outlet to global franchise.

"No excuses," he says, and points his laser at the chart projected onto the wall. "We were here—" the red dot finds a peak "—and now we're here." It moves down a decline that ends above March's gaping maw. I think of coal chutes, water slides, the end of evolution. "I want answers," he says. "And. I. Want. Them. Now."

I stare at his penis. It's funny how the naughty bits draw us. Penis, vagina. Our private place, our power over life. Some people name theirs. I suspect our CEO is one of them. Jack, I'm thinking, or Harry. Something mundane.

Now he's droning about distribution bottlenecks and labor costs. I imagine his penis talking, tiny face, oblong mouth, words dribbling out—*splat, splat.* How am I supposed to take this seriously? I glance around the table. Rapt attention, but I'm betting none of us could repeat a thing he said.

The Beast They Do Not See

They run in circles, faster and faster, each chasing the other, chasing themselves. "Slow down!" the centermaster screams. "You're straining the rods, you're twisting the chain." They move too rapidly for warnings to catch them, too energetically for childish brains to understand.

A crack, a snap, and the center post topples. Gone is the restraint that applies purpose to their power. The runners fly off at angles, pinballs unleashed upon the city of man.

Splat! goes one, Splash! another, as flesh intersects brick as plate glass cuts them clean. Blood drenches desiccated gutters ill-designed to handle such sludge. Mounds of flesh and shattered bone. Children, they were children, are they children still? Is innocence forever?

"We don't understand," inventors lament. "We designed it to harness entropic energy. This device should have saved us from the desert consequence of our prior inventions."

"You did this!" parents shout. "You sacrificed our progeny to fuel your evil intent. All we wanted was tomorrow today."

A thunderous thud, a skirling wind. There, on the horizon, the beast, the lion, the inevitable force. No compassion in that gaze, no sympathy in that soul.

Concrete cracks. The broken center post spins around.

"A sign!" the centermaster screams. "We must strive to comprehend."

"No." Inventors, on their knees, ears pressed to the ground: "The water is coming if you will only hear."

"No." Parents stand tall, eyes lifted to the haze. "Our children are there, if you will only look."

A piston step shakes bedrock. A swishing tail throws sandstorms. And, still, they do not see.

ORIGINALLY APPEARED IN *APOCRYPHA AND ABSTRACTIONS*

A Tallish Tale

So there was this tall guy, and he had this *Ziploc®* bag filled with dirt. It wasn't actually full, but an empty portion is useless in a tale like this, so imagine it was full. He comes to the door—it was Sunday right after church—and he rings the bell and leans down and smiles for the peephole and straightens his tie, and eventually I do answer because… what else would I do on a sunny Sunday with a well-dressed man standing outside my door? I had a successful career, SUV, HBO, but I didn't have a man, and the sermon that morning had been on the emptiness of a life without a man, how Jesus lit up Mary Magdalene's purpose by letting her wash his feet. Or something. I wasn't really listening. We had this report due at work and the data validation aspect was proving to be a bastard.

And this man, as the door opens, he says: "Good day to you ma'am. How much will you give me for this primo soil?" So I'm thinking, *Who buys dirt? I have a gardenful of dirt. I have a terrarium filled with dirt*—well maybe not full, but full enough for the purpose of analogy.

I must have been staring, because the next I knew he had my hand. It was strong, his grip, and warm and kind and full, and I was kind of taken in by it.

"How much?" he said, and the bag lifted between me and the sun. Light shown through its pores. Light scattered a thought, how diamond is a type of dirt too, how everything is dirt in the end.

"I don't know," I said. "How much do you want?"

"That depends on how you value the things you encounter in life."

"I don't want to overpay," I said. A blush warmed my face. He chuckled, and I felt less embarrassed.

"What makes it worthwhile?" I said. "Does it come from a special place?"

"You mean like Grandmother's grave? Einstein's ashes? Harry Potter's potting soil?"

"I guess."

He lowered the bag. Our eyes met. His were serious brown with a touch of twinkle.

"If it helps," he said, "I put it on eBay yesterday."

"And?"

"It's priceless," he said. "Not a single offer."

"Oh." Was I disappointed?

"Look," he said. "Here's how importantly I view this transaction." And he peeled the plastic zipper. The opening puckered. I thought of his lips and how it might feel to kiss them.

He tilted the bag. "If you don't buy this soil, I'll spill it, let the wind and the world take it, and it will no longer belong to either of us."

"That doesn't seem… I mean…"

"Indeed," he said. "It would be a great loss." He tipped the bag until the first motes sprinkled down.

I stopped him. What kind of ending would it be, had I not?

He looked into me. I looked into him.

"Will you take a check?"

ORIGINALLY APPEARED IN *PURE SLUSH*

Minnows

We used to squat by the tub and scoop minnows from our bathwater by the dozens. Shelly liked to eat them whole, but I was strictly catch and release. She called it a cruel kindness to submit them to such treatment.

"You're inflicting something much worse than digestion on those poor fish, Charlie."

"And what might that be?"

"Hope."

Years later she asks if I remember that day.

Of course I remember. "You ate those fish and you told me how cruel it was to let them go."

"Was I wrong? Did you do them any favors?"

The question makes me uncomfortable. I recall the minnows' struggles as soap suds overcame them. Gills suck, torpedo bodies roll, ballast fails, spines arch. I feel their agony as they call out in that silent voice: *It's your fault, Charlie. Death is not painful, but hope? That hurts more than anything.*

Shelly presses her hands to her stomach. "For all you know, Charlie, the fish I swallowed are still alive. Jonah and the whale in reverse."

"It's been years," I say. "Do they even live this long?"

Shelly sinks onto her knees, tilts her chin. Her mouth opens wide. Her breath is dank.

Heart pounding, I lean in.

ORIGINALLY APPEARED IN *NEW FLASH FICTION*

Scum

"Ahoy!" the fisherman said. He shifted forward, nudging the boat a few inches across the pond's mossy surface. I thought of the way Marina had pushed that lima bean through a scum of spaghetti sauce last night. I shouldn't have said anything then and I wasn't about to repeat the mistake now.

"I said Ahoy!" the fisherman said. He had outfitted his rowboat's prow with a stork. It wasn't a real stork, but a wooden one, a prop from some redneck trailer yard. We have a lot of those out here.

Now he was reeling in his line, the bobber hopping toward him. "What's yer name, boy?"

Javier Rodriguez. People around here call me JR.

"Are ye' deaf?" He packed his pole into the boat and stood. The boat rocked beneath him. I wanted him to fall, but it was good he didn't. I would have had to jump in and rescue him. "Are ye' simple?"

"I just broke up with my girlfriend, okay?" Of course, my line chose that moment to snap taut and bow the pole down to the water's surface. I nearly dropped it. Whatever took that lure was plenty big.

"That's it, boy. Hold on." The fisherman pumped his fist. "Play it out."

I let the fish have some line.

"Give 'er some line!" the fisherman yelled.

I pulled and reeled.

"Pull 'er in some. Tire 'er out."

26

The line zagged away. When it relaxed, I reeled again. There was a flash beneath the scum.

The fisherman fitted an oar to the oarlock. He rowed once, twice. The prow of the boat twisted toward me. He was getting awfully close to where the fish was.

"Don't cut my line," I warned. That was how I lost Marina. Some jerk-she wouldn't say a name-had cut my hold on her.

The fisherman frowned. "Why not? This's a private pond. You got no right to fish here."

"My mom works for the owner," I said. What I didn't say was that the owner hadn't given me permission to fish.

"Hey, you're that *Mexican* boy, ain't ya?"

Rage flooded me. I let go with one hand and clenched my fist. In the same instant, the fish pulled hard. The rod slipped. I lunged. The reel screamed. I caught the handle and yanked the pole up and toward me.

The fish leapt, a glorious beast. It seemed to fly in slow motion, tail arched, droplets flung. My breath caught. My eyes closed.

There was no splash.

When I looked again, the fisherman was calmly removing my lure from the fish's jaw. It flapped so hard the boat jiggled, but that didn't faze the fisherman. He worked the barb free and dropped my line onto the water. Peering at me through steady eyes, he slapped the fish hard against the boat side. I witnessed its final gasp, recalling my own mouth spasming against the pillow last night.

Water clapped lightly. I heard the quiet wheeze of the fisherman breathing.

"I asked you a question," he said, lifting the fish by its gill. Fifteen inches dangled from that bony finger. "Are ya Mexican, boy, or ain't ya?"

I looked at my hand, too brown for a tan.

"Well?" the fisherman said.

"My father..." My voice faltered.

"Yeah? Your father what?" His expression held equal parts taunt and ridicule. "Out with it, *boy*. You want your fish or not?"

"My father came to this country with nothing."

The fisherman laughed. "That ain't exactly true, now, is it. He brought his seed. He brought his laziness."

I wondered if the pond would support me, if I might walk out there and take what was mine. I glared at my feet. My shoes were muddy.

"Ya got no right to be here, boy." There was a splash. An oar slapped and gulped. I looked up to see the rowboat retreating.

The fish lay dead on the scum, its belly reflecting white.

Trickle Down

They've taken to sharing a body, these survivors of themselves, these human frames stitched into a mutilated mass of flesh and hair, sinew and bone. Single-minded, guts tapped into a labyrinth sewer at their core, they chew toward the horizon. Mouths of various sizes consume trees, grass, a beehive laced with honey, birds' nests, wolves too proud to retreat, horses with broken legs, groundhog families in their dens, an eggshell colored purple.

Entire buildings go down the group gullet now: glass shards, twisted metal, houses with tarpaper roofs. The Boys and Girls Club of greater Dayton.

They pause after a planetarium. A belch blows fetid from their mouths. Will they stop? Have they consumed enough?

No. With a grumbling shudder, the flesh-mass moves again, the ground behind it shiny with the residue of their digestion.

ORIGINALLY APPEARED IN *POLLUTO*

Good Deeds

Ronnie was lugging a suitcase full of money to the bank when he encountered a beggar hunched by a light pole.

"Hey, friend," the beggar said. "Can you spare some change?" He shook a Styrofoam cup half-filled with coins.

Ronnie smiled his infectious smile. "Of course I can, but I won't." He straightened his tie. "Have you considered getting a job? Then you could buy all the coffee and food you want."

Confusion passed over the beggar's face, quickly replaced by surprise.

"Why, that's a great idea, Mister. Why didn't I think of it?" He struggled to his feet and hurried to the nearest business to fill out an application.

Ronnie poured the contents of the man's cup into his suitcase. *Waste not, want not.* He continued down the sidewalk, whistling a merry tune.

A woman in black leather pants and a tube top stepped out of shadow. Her lips glowed with pink lipstick. "You looking for a good time?"

"Always," Ronnie said. "Is there a fair in town?"

The woman nodded toward a ragged awning. *Hotel Malchanceux.* Beneath it, a glass door hung open from a bent hinge. A sign proclaimed, *$10 an hour.*

"Oh," Ronnie said. "Rather than selling your body to strangers, why not marry a good man?"

Understanding bloomed in the woman's eyes. "Of course. How about you, sir? You seem good and kind."

"I do, don't I?" Ronnie shrugged. "Alas, I'm taken. My wife is picking up my son from private school even now." He glanced meaningfully at his Rolex. "Why not try a Christian dating service?"

"Oh, I will!" The woman leaned in and kissed Ronnie's cheek. "How can I repay you?"

Ronnie sniffed stale perfume. "Five minutes of my time," he said. "Twenty dollars ought to cover it."

"Oh," she said. She reached between her breasts and produced a folded twenty-dollar bill, pressed it into Ronnie's hand, and hustled off to find an internet terminal.

Ronnie slid the bill into his suitcase. His gaze tracked to the hotel. He walked beneath the awning.

An unshaven man stood behind a counter. "Help you?" he said. He had one good eye. The other was as broken as the door.

"I can help you," Ronnie said. "This building is badly run down. Have you considered fixing it up to attract an upscale clientele?"

The man squinted. "That does make sense. I'll get right on it."

"Excellent," Ronnie said. He reached into his vest and produced a business card. *Renovations. No job too large or small.* "Call this number and tell them Ronnie sent you."

"I will," the man said. He took the card.

Ronnie exited the hotel. He would receive a referral fee, of course, but mainly it was the good deed that motivated him.

He continued toward the bank. He had not gone ten steps before a woman with a bleeding lip ran into him. A cell phone dropped to the ground.

"Help me, mister. Please. He broke my phone."

Ronnie pried her fingers from his arm. "Have you considered marriage counseling?"

31

"We're not married." She peered past his shoulder.

"You should be," Ronnie said.

"Of course," the woman said. "That makes sense. We'll get married, and then we can go to counseling. Thank you so much." She strolled away, window shopping for an engagement ring.

Ronnie picked up the cell phone. It was likely repairable. He continued.

Next it was a drunk sprawled on the sidewalk. "Have you tried soft drinks?" A man with Tourette's told him to fuck himself. "Cognitive Behavior Therapy will clear that right up." A girl tried to steal his wallet. "Girl Scouts," Ronnie recommended. She promised to deliver ten boxes of free cookies. He accepted her shoes as collateral.

By the time he reached the bank he had spent his good will. Even a compassionate man has limits.

"Next?" a blonde called. Ronnie walked to her station and plopped the suitcase on the ledge.

"I want to make a deposit." He opened the case to reveal stacks tens and twenties, wadded ones, food stamps, a skim of stray change, a pair of shoes and a broken cell phone.

The girl stared.

"Well?" he said.

"Could you come back tomorrow? We're shorthanded. Jessie's sick and Marge had to leave early. Her husband's in the hospital."

"That's not my problem," Ronnie said. "I wish to speak to your manager."

The teller talked into an intercom. "He'll see you." She nodded toward a glass cubicle.

Ronnie carried his suitcase across the lobby. *All the good I do for this city*, he thought, *and this is my reward.* He sat in a lobby chair and watched the minutes tick past. Presently the bank manager summoned him. Ronnie knew him from golf outings, primarily.

"What's the problem?" the manager said.

"You're understaffed," Ronnie said. "There's no one to sort my deposit." He opened the suitcase on a shining mahogany desk. The bank manager whistled under his breath.

"Ten thousand, six hundred, thirty five dollars, sixty eight cents," Ronnie said. "I'll want the shoes and cell phone and other miscellaneous items in a safe deposit box."

"Certainly," the manager said. He filled out a deposit slip with bold strokes of a fountain pen.

Ronnie nodded. "As for your staffing problem, have you considered hiring more tellers? There are plenty of people looking for work."

"That's a fine notion," the manager said. "I can use the money in your suitcase to pay them."

Ronnie gave a cold stare. "If that's a joke, it's a poor one. Might I remind you, this bank is *not* too big to fail."

"I understand," the manager said. Sweat gleamed from his upper lip. "I'll hire the extra tellers post-haste and pay them from the pension fund."

Ronnie allowed his smile to emerge. "There's a good man. See what we can accomplish when we apply ourselves? No problem is so large we cannot solve it together."

Global Warming

We've been treading water for decades, surrounded by people with flotation devices, pool toys, inner tubes, couch cushions. Denial. Anything will do in this time of Global Warming. Does it matter? At times your saturated hand in mine is enough. We have that. Our crinkles match trough to ridge, ridge to trough.

And then I look into your eyes and they are dead. Not in the literal sense, but in the sense of endless repetition. Waves, that momentary lift, the swell, the falling like a roller coaster smoothed safe. I feel a warmth in my trunks and realize that I am peeing into this endless soup, we all are. Once upon a time, we did not do this. Once upon a time we cared. So goes the myth.

Your pool donut has lost air. We have always taken turns blowing it up. Someday we will run out of breath. We will sink into the depths and never be seen. Isn't *that* what matters?

A glint in the distance, a shimmer of white. Someone is carving through this jetsam on a sailboard. I squint, hoping to see the rider. Maybe it's Al Gore. There's a violence to it, a chop and surge. My heart pounds in cadence. A muffled scream, a splash. *Pop!* goes a raft. Blood sprays from fresh-cleaved flesh. The sailboard slaps and jumps.

Around us people are awakening. Water thrashes as they kick and paddle, but there's nowhere to go, no space to maneuver.

And still, the chaos comes, the salt spray and the blood.

Originally appeared in *Bodega*

Sons and Fathers

This is the book of the killing of Jesus Christ, the son of David, the son of Abraham.

Isaac killed Abraham; and Jacob killed Isaac; and Judas and his brethren killed Jacob; And Phares and Zara of Thamar killed Judas; and Esrom killed Phares; and Aram killed Esrom; And Aminadab killed Aram; and Naasson killed Aminadab; and Salmon killed Naasson; And Booz of Rachab killed Salmon; and Obed of Ruth killed Booz; and Jesse killed Obed; And David the king killed Jesse; and Solomon of her that had been the wife of Urias killed David the king; And Roboam killed Solomon; and Abia killed Roboam; and Asa killed Abia; And Josaphat killed Asa; and Joram killed Josaphat; and Ozias killed Joram; And Joatham killed Ozias; and Achaz killed Joatham; and Ezekias killed Achaz; And Manasses killed Ezekias; and Amon killed Manasses; and Josias killed Amon; Jechonias and his brethren killed Josias. And after they were brought to Babylon, Salathiel killed Jechonias; and Zorobabel killed Salathiel; And Abiud killed Zorobabel; and Eliakim killed Abiud; and Azor killed Eliakim; And Sadoc killed Azor; and Achim killed Sadoc; and Eliud killed Achim; And Eleazar killed Eliud; and Matthan killed Eleazar; and Jacob killed Matthan; And Joseph the husband of Mary, of whom was born Jesus, who is called Christ, killed Jacob.

And we said unto God, "Why hast thou created a world of such murderous nature, O Father?" And He said unto us, "You have eaten of the fruit of the tree that was in the midst of my garden. Thus shall it ever be, my children, that the son murders his father by inches, and the father gives life to his son. The husk must crack so that the seed may flourish."

ORIGINALLY APPEARED IN *CAPER LITERARY JOURNAL*

Heart

My father was still in the middle of our driveway. He'd been there since last fall, face pale, blood drained down into the core of him, into the mounds of fat that were his middle, the flesh-logs of his folded thighs.

"It's my heart," he said. Sunlight caught the lonely wave crest of white hair that lifted from his scalp.

"It's not your heart," Mom said. She swung a grocery bag past his head. "It's your will."

Why can't it be both? I was in middle school, but my ideas ran old for my age.

A second grocery bag caught Dad square in the back. He jolted forward. Fat compressed against bone, bone pressed into asphalt, a chain reaction.

"Help me," he gasped. Hands clasped and unclasped in time with his ragged breaths.

"Help yourself," Mom said. She carried groceries across the patio to the sliding glass door and unlocked it. I thought of the coolness inside—we had central air—and debated whether to follow her or stay behind.

"Please," Dad said. His spine was bent like a nail. He turned his face sideways.

I pulled his shoulders as hard as I could.

"That's better," he said. "Thank you." His hand reached but mine had already moved, and he ended up patting his own collarbone.

"My heart," he said.

36

"It's like Mom says. You don't try."

"I do!" He spread his arms incoherently. "All my life, all my passion, everything for..." Sobs shook him. Snot drooled from his mouth and nose. I left him in the harsh sun and went inside.

By summer's end, his scalp was cracked and bleeding. His shoulders had rounded into pillows. Now his stomach spilled over his thighs onto the driveway. We thought maybe the birds were feeding him, or squirrels.

"Enablers!" Mom would grumble on her way to or from the garage. It was not easy to get the car around Dad, but she'd learned how to cut the wheel just right.

"Why won't you get up?" I asked. "It can't be pleasant out here." I thought of the bats we saw outside each night. Did they nibble his ears?

His breath wheezed. He reached feebly.

"You have to do it yourself. Mom says if I help, you won't learn your lesson."

He pressed one hand between his breasts. "Broken." More croak than a word. His bloodshot eyes begged.

"If your heart quit, you'd be dead." I wasn't stupid. "It's not that easy. There's this girl in school who lived in a trailer for a year. *She* didn't stop trying. She even got a C+ on the last Algebra quiz."

Dad's eyes closed. His shoulders jiggled. His lips were cracked like the ground in Mom's garden. I went inside and got a bottled water from the fridge.

"Is that for him?" Mom sat by the window. I could not read her expression. "What'd he tell you?"

"Nothing," I said. "I just... I thought maybe he needs a drink. Maybe if we give him a drink—"

"We can't coddle," Mom said. Her eyes fixed on mine. "It will never end."

"He just sits there."

"His choice."

"I know, Mom, but why can't we help him? Just a little."

She shook her face. "Do you want to spend the rest of your life enabling others? It's sink or swim in the real world, darling."

My thigh tensed. My hand reached for the door handle, then fell back. I walked to the fridge and replaced the bottle on its shelf. Outside, Father sank inch by inch into the tar.

And Then He Moved

Michael's father was a billionaire, self-made and proud. He owned factories and distribution chains, flower shops and funeral homes. He ate caviar for breakfast and brushed his teeth with champagne.

It was the night before Michael went off to college that they sat down to have "the talk". Michael had known this was coming for months, but it was still disconcerting. The secrets a father shared could make or break a son's life. Michael wasn't certain he was ready.

His father nodded to a chair across the polished desk. Michael sat. Sweat collected in his armpits. Did it show?

"I came from humble roots," his father began.

"I know," Michael said. "We're very proud —"

"Let me finish."

"Yes, sir." Michael gripped the chair arms.

His father nodded. "My father, your grandfather, was barely a millionaire, and yet he was a wise man in his way. I'm going to share with you the advice he gave me when I was your age." He leaned forward. Michael leaned forward too, stomach packed with butterflies and bees.

"Beware the killer drug," his father said. "Your friends will tell you it lifts you up, but it will only take you down. Do not reduce the lifetime of responsible wealth I have amassed to mere moments of joy, Michael."

"I won't, sir." Which drug did his father mean? There were so many, and he had already experimented with a few.

"You will know it by its cloying smell," his father said. "The sweetness on your tongue. You will know it by the smiles of others, their fond embraces and shining eyes. One sniff, one taste, Michael, and you are lost. Do you understand?"

"I think so, Father." *Cocaine?* Some of Michael's friends had done a line or two.

"Good," his father said. He leaned back and slapped his thighs. "Good."

"Just to be certain," Michael said. "This is cocaine you speak of, correct?"

His father's trimmed brows pulled together. "No, Michael, cocaine is fine. It helped me through many twenty-hour days." He sighed. "No drug should be abused, of course. You must retain mastery of your appetite."

"Yes, sir. Is it heroine, then?" That horse was said to kick harder than cocaine.

His father shook his head.

"LSD?" A hippy drug. His father despised hippies.

Another negative. Michael tensed. How could he run his father's companies if he could not even understand a simple thing?

"The drug I speak of," his father said, "is TLC."

Michael's gut went cold. "Marijuana?" He was already lost. He'd smoked pot, ingested it, rolled it into his cigarettes.

"Not THC," his father said, "though I do not approve of that, either. Have you smoked the stuff?"

Michael stared through the window.

"Well, stop," his father said. "It undercuts drive and turns you sloppy."

"Yes, sir." He would miss that soothing smoke, the slow, steady stroll of conscious thought.

"The drug I mean, is love, Michael, empathy, sympathy, affection. Do not partake of that emotion, or you will be lost. Now, do you see? Will you heed my advice, son? As I heeded my father's?"

Michael sat, unmoving, expressionless, as grains of understanding trickled down. This explained so much about his father, his mother, everything.

"There's a good man." His father checked his diamond-crusted Rolex. Their appointment was at an end.

Michael stood on unsteady legs, and walked to the exit. He turned the knob, swung the door open—so smooth and uncomplaining on that substantial hinge—and stopped. He couldn't help himself.

"Does this mean, Father, that you do not love me?"

His father's lips pursed full. "What do you want from me, Michael, an empire or a kiss?"

For the longest time Michael waited halfway in, halfway out. And then he moved.

ORIGINALLY IN *AND THEN HE MOVED, A SCARS ANTHOLOGY*

Silly Hats

The line must be a mile long, but it is the only way in. I take my place behind a man in a top hat with a sparkled wand shoved through the crown.

"You look ridiculous," I say, touching my Stetson for emphasis. I'm going to be a country singer.

Top Hat turns as if to acknowledge a car backfire or an ex-wife with a restraining order. "We shall see." There's a twinkle in his eyes that reminds me uncomfortably of Dad. He's the reason I'm here in the *Chase Your Dream* line instead of at college earning a place in the "real" world. He's always telling me to stand tall, cut my hair, wear a clean shirt. *Behave, belong, be straight.* Well, I can't. I never could. I've been gay since the day I watched *Jason and the Argonauts* in Cinevision, and the only clean shirt I have is in the laundry.

Top Hat turns back into place, just another man in another line. He's tall, though, I'll give him that. His shadow is tiny, scrunched and deformed around his feet. I'm going to be the opposite of him. I'm going to stand on stage with that spotlight beaming down and my shadow will stretch around the world.

I'll have my pick of gay groupies, sprinkle in a blushing girl or two for spice. A thrill runs up my spine. I think of the guy ahead of me on all fours, grunting as I thrust inside him. I think of my hands clamped to the brim of that stupid hat, pulling it tighter and tighter until his eyes stop twinkling. It's not like me—I'm the submissive one, haven't even actually come out to my parents yet—but that's about to change. I imagine the last note of my audition fading, the sweet tone of my voice hanging for that instant between anonymity and fame. The spotlight is thick with

42

motes, so heavy and slow moving I count them like stars in the night sky, wants and wishes and equality. I could count them all, if only this moment will last forever.

The line moves one stride, two, three, a dozen. The studio has swallowed the next batch. I glance at the sun. Will it last until I am swallowed too? I should not have slept in. That reminds me of Dad. I turn my thoughts off.

The sun moves overhead, and I drift, drift drift...

Two thuggish guys block the entrance. One is a skinhead, the other sports a Mohawk, big-muscled men with washboard abs and soulless stares. One is gay, the other probably straight. I can tell this from subtle differences in posture.

I edge closer to the gay one.

"Bug off," he says. His voice is like gravel. Heavy smoker, I think. I scan his forearms but see no scars.

"He's with me," Top Hat says. "He's my son. We're an act." The straight bouncer frowns. The gay one looks me over.

"I don't even know him," I say. Anger boils into my voice until I sound hysterical. "I wouldn't be caught dead with this guy."

"Suit yerself," the straight bouncer says. He pushes the door open.

Top Hat casts a sad glance my way and moves through into darkness. The sparkles in his wand wink and die. I squint but can't make out much inside.

"Scram," the gay bouncer says.

"What? I'm next." My stomach gurgles.

"You heard 'im." The other bouncer steps forward. "Scram, loser. You ain't welcome here."

"Is it because I'm... homosexual?"

Gay bouncer rolls his eyes. "Read it and weep, retard." He points to a sign above the door. *Silly Hats Only.*

The other bouncer shrugs. "That's what the judges want."

I gather myself. "When is Country Singer Day?"

The straight one laughs. "Second Tuesday every week. Are you kidding me?"

"No," I say steadily. "I'm not kidding. I will not be deterred." In my head, I hear Father say, *Our greatest weakness lies in giving up. Thomas Edison.* Of course, Dad was talking about taking my driving test a third time, but I've always believed it applies to other matters too.

"Get a load of dis guy," the straight one says to everyone around us. "Says he don't want to be a turd, but way too late for that, right?"

"You're holding up the line," a chick in a feathered hat complains.

"No," I shout. "*You're* holding up the line." I stab my finger at her, then at a short dude wearing Mickey Mouse ears, an older guy draped head to toe in balloons. "You're the log jam. You walk around like robots in an assembly line, you let jerks like these two tell you what to be. Well, I'm not putting up with it. I was born to sing, I'm meant to be a country singer, and I will—"

The straight bouncer grabs me. "You ain't meant for shit, Sherlock. You think Jamie and me was born to stand by some damn metal door and let in a bunch 'a loons to prance on some electrifed stage? You think that's my calling? You think this is what God intended me to do?"

"Maybe it's all you're good for." Even as the words leave me, I know it's a mistake.

His fist crashes my jaw. Sparks everywhere. My legs go wobbly. I crumple into a squat. A boot slams my stomach, launching an explosive grunt. I sprawl onto someone's feet.

Sunlight turns into crystal shards. I taste blood. I reach up. The Stetson is gone.

Panic seizes me. I can't breathe. My lungs won't expand no matter how I suck. I clutch and writhe. My face goes cold.

Balloon Man kneels beside me. "Relax. Don't struggle. It will come to you."

But it won't. It won't. There's a void inside me. Nothing will fill it. Not air, not love, nothing.

"You'll be okay," Balloon Man says. He presses a business card into my hand. "Call me tomorrow. I'm a lawyer." He stands, eyes drawn to the door opening to admit another gaggle of dream chasers.

I clutch at his hand. *It's not the stage you want but the applause.* I feel giddy with sudden revelation. *We're born to breathe, to eat and drink and love each other.* I know that. I know everything in this heartbeat between living and dying. Nothing is natural, nothing is real, nothing matters but the next breath, the next caress, the next word.

Balloon Man straightens his silly hat. For a moment, I imagine Father gazing down. And then he is gone, sucked into the darkness beyond the door.

Dance it Down

Igor is one of the beautiful people. Even his deep thoughts rainbow, his eyes interpret miracles in the everyday. Let's put Igor on this pedestal.

Esdaile smells of garlic, the creases in her hands, her parchment lips. She is a vampire huntress, a woman with passionate need to true the sublime. She belongs on the chessboard. Black, I think. Let her move herself to white.

The cat? Drop it, shoo it, boy/girl. We cannot have it here. Allergy. Dolphin friendly tuna costs too much. The claws.

The rest of these are Greek. They do not speak English, and therefore do not matter. Leave them on the pile.

"Get ready to rrrrrrrrruuuuuummmmmmmba!"

Pedal boy/girl. The scene demands your energy.

Twitch. Igor drops onto the apron. He lifts his butt and twerks. Oh, how clever! Faster, boy/girl, animate them both.

Esdaile slides, electric-wise. Her hips gyrate. Cha-cha-cha, black to white to white to white, she diagonals toward the fringe. Igor turns, his face a rock, a potato. Esdaile eyes the crevices. A tongue-point licks.

Keep pedaling, boy/girl, electrify it all. We are *not* robots living forward, but mannequins rotated in reverse. Our torsos chime with heart, our eyes are paint and shadow.

Fingers extend. Sparks. Oh, this could get interesting. This could sex. Conception. Creation dance. Close your eyes boy/girl. You are too young.

Esdaile kneads Igor's hunch. His mouth opens, a crooning sound. She is perfect to him, he is perfect to her, the pinnacle of human existence here on the fringe of the chessboard, here in the light of our dreams.

Pedal faster, faster, faster...

They're both twerking now, jerking now, blood splatter, *pop-pop-pop*.

Damn, boy/girl, we forgot the Greeks. They form ranks along the sideways, a shooting squad. Stop the bike, cease the flood.

Too late. Igor's down. Esdaile collapses onto him, dress a tattered umbrella. White squares blacken with blood. Those filthy Greeks. They had their myths, why can't they leave us ours?

I'm sorry boy/girl. I forgot the rule. Language is no barrier. I should have known. We should have penned them or peppered them or pulled apart their skin. I was impatient. Even beautiful people break.

Close your eyes. Close your ears, your mouth. Pretend this never was. Un-experience if you can.

I know you can't.

Oh, boy/girl, I'm sorry. It was a game, Romeo and Juliette twisted. I was being clever. I didn't mean to abuse your light.

ORIGINALLY APPEARED IN *HERMENEUTIC CHAOS*

Across the River

Silence. Marcy eased her hands away from her ears. Gunfire had sounded throughout the cold night, leading her to huddle in a nest of cardboard next to a dumpster. Light filtered into the alley through a haze of wood smoke. Half the town must be aflame. Fortunately, the buildings facing the blind alley were brick.

She found her revolver and stood carefully. Her back ached as it always did in the morning. She touched her toes. Stretching helped a little. Ibuprofen would help more, but it was up to twenty bucks a pill.

Somewhere a bird called out. A sniper answered with a single crackling shot. Marcy's stomach clenched. Silence returned.

If Elitist snipers controlled the street, she was in for trouble. Marcy's rag-tag clothing marked her as underclass. In truth, she held no longer held political views after years of war. It was enough to survive.

James had been political. Oh, the fire in his eyes when he marched off with his mates to carry the battle to the steel cities. They carried inferior weapons, followed an inferior strategy, but their passion had been undeniable. That was something the cold-eyed Elitists would never match.

A footstep echoed. Marcy dived back to her nest. She pulled cardboard around herself.

"I know you're here," a voice said. "My sensor is attuned to your heat signature."

Marcy clutched the revolver to her chest. Even unloaded, it was something at least.

"There's no need to hide." A soft sigh. "I'm quite harmless."

Marcy risked a peek. Across the alley, a man leaned heavily on a metal cane. His uniform was crisply ironed, his hat angled down his forehead. Shadow covered much of his face, but his chin was firm and clean shaven.

"You're... blind?" Marcy stammered.

"More or less." His mouth made a quick smile. He seemed tired now that Marcy looked closer. "My name is Alphonse." He removed his hat. His eyelids reminded Marcy of sinkholes before they opened up to swallow a road or a house.

"I'm Marcy." She snapped her mouth shut. How many times had James told her not to volunteer information? Not to answer questions under interrogation? Elitist minds were quenched in cold logic, their emotions worn flat by exposure to their beloved machines. They would use anything you told them to kill your friends and family.

Alphonse pulled something from his uniform pocket. Marcy flinched. It was only a cellophane pack. She watched as he worked it open and extracted a cigarette.

"Do you smoke?" He tossed the cigarette. It landed with a patter and rolled onto the lowest piece of Marcy's cardboard.

Her body responded. Warmth spread through her chest and arms. Saliva leaked into her mouth. Addiction had been an Elitist strategy: hook the underclass on nicotine then manipulate ingredients to kill.

A matchbook followed.

Marcy stared. It would be ludicrous to smoke that. Yet her body ached with need for the smooth feel of smoke in her lungs, bleeding through her nostrils, the pinch on her taste buds.

"Go ahead," Alphonse said. "It's not been altered." His empty eyes watched.

Why not? I'm dead anyway. She jammed the cigarette between her lips. It took three strikes to get a match lit. She considered tossing it onto the cardboard and using the resulting smokescreen to escape. but where would she go? Snipers watching the street, her family dead or gone...

She lit up. Serenity swarmed through her. She exhaled through her nose.

"Okay," Alphonse said. "Here's the deal, Marcy. You are the last of the resistance in this town."

Last? Marcy blinked. The town had been well populated yesterday. She'd played cards with Ernie over at the drug store while his wife tended the all-day stew pot. Several others had come in during the game to buy a helping.

"You're lying," she said.

"We've never lied," Alphonse said, "not about the challenges facing our society, the need for education, the ethical dimensions of our research. Certainly not this."

Marcy sniffed. "All you Elitists know is lying. You twist the world around to your theories and take away our freedoms."

Alphonse leaned onto his cane. "This is not the time for politics. Accept that you are the last and listen to my offer."

"Or?" Marcy said, jabbing the cigarette toward him.

"We'll kill you too," Alphonse said. The flatness of the response was like a slap. Marcy crushed the cigarette stub beneath her boot.

"We propose a truce," Alphonse said. "We want you to carry terms across the river."

"That's forty miles," Marcy said.

"So it is." Alphonse brushed his uniform sleeve. "Here are our terms. First, we agree to grant your people safe haven west of the river. You are free to live and die as you please, so long as you do not interfere with our research. Will you carry our terms?"

"Why should I?"

"Why shouldn't you? Be brave for once in your life."

A curse leapt to Marcy's tongue. She bit it back. Would it be cowardice or bravery to walk out into that street on a blind man's promise, to carry potential peace through a wilderness of snipers and wild animals? She wished James were here.

"How do I know you're telling the truth?" she said. "How do I know you speak for your kind."

"My kind," Alphonse spat. "That's the problem, Marcy, you only see in black and white, have and have not, we and they."

"What do you see?" she said.

"Nothing." He smiled. He stood straighter. "What is your choice? There are settlements closer to the river. Surely we'll find someone with a spine in one of them."

Marcy's gut went tight. She wanted to leap across the alley and tear her adversary's face off, coat her fingers with blood. But that was a chump's game. Elitists valued their individual lives only slightly more than their machines. She could kill this guy and another would replace him.

"I'll do it," she said. "But it's not going to turn out like you think. We'll build a better world, we'll hunt and fish and—"

"Procreate," Alphonse said. "You'll overpopulate, overhunt, overfish, over cultivate, over everything until your side of the river is a desolate wasteland."

Marcy blushed, thinking of the awkward sex she'd had with Ernie. "Yes, of course we'll have babies. While you die off. You're too busy making machines to make love."

Alphonse nodded toward the alley mouth. "You have safe passage. You may pick up whatever supplies you need in the stores across the street. Do not dally."

"I won't," Marcy said. "I'll be gone before your snipers can site their rifles."

Alphonse muttered something under his breath.

Marcy bristled. "What?"

"I said, Godspeed," Alphonse said. "I hope you're right that you and your kind will build a better world. I hope you will learn restraint." He started toward the street but stopped at the alley's mouth. "We have our own lessons to learn, Marcy. If there is a God, pray that at least one of our peoples succeeds."

Spring Fashion

"Let me see," Carol says. She's younger than her sister and anxious to catch up.

Emily gives a sour look, then changes her mind and smiles. "Hold your nose." She sits on the bed and rolls down her stocking.

"It's not like I can't smell it already," Carol says. For days a faint odor has followed her sister, like almonds rolled in shit. She masks it with perfume, but it's there if you know where to look.

"Suit yourself." The sock comes off. The smell intensifies. An Ace bandage has been wound around Emily's foot. Her toes are deep blue, edging toward black.

"How do you walk?" Carol says. So far Emily has everyone convinced it's just a minor sprain.

"You do what you have to," Emily says. "And I don't want you telling them anything, understand?" Carol nods immediately. *Them*, of course, is their parents.

"Can I touch?" Carol says.

Emily rolls her eyes. She lifts her foot from the floor.

Carol reaches tentatively. "Does it hurt?"

"I don't feel a thing." Emily wipes her mouth with the back of a hand.

Carol touches her sister's big toe. The flesh is cold and hard, not like skin at all. She pulls away. A thrill of terror runs down her spine. For the first time, she understands how dangerous her sister's obsession has become.

"Can I finish dressing now?" Emily says.

Carol shakes her head. "I want to see more."

"Can't this wait until after school?"

"Now," Carol says. "Show me or I'm telling Mom." To her utter shock, she means it. This was a game until now. Could Emily hide the infection from their parents? Once the operation was done it would be too late for them to stop her. Emily's lower leg would become a graceful arc, her foot spring metal. That was the plan. Now, Carol is having second thoughts.

Emily blows a sigh, but there's a hint of satisfaction too. She wants to show off for her little sister. She hikes up her pants leg, revealing metal wire embedded in the glossy white skin of her calf. She unwinds the bandage. The smell makes Carol retch. She breathes through her mouth. Emily's foot is glazed dark blue. Purple veins reach up her ankle.

"Almost done," she grates between clenched teeth.

"I thought you said it didn't hurt," Carol says.

"Everything in life hurts," Emily says, "even fashion." She touches the dented skin. "This is where the doctors will be forced to amputate. Enough stump for a good prosthesis fit."

Carol can't decide whether she's horrified or excited. "What color will you get?"

"Probably pink," Emily says. "That's what Janine got, and Marie too. Boys love it." She looks thoughtful. "I'll get purple for my tread, though. I don't want to get lost in the crowd." She presses one end of the bandage to her flesh, and winds the first layer around.

Carol watches open-mouthed, as her sister's secret disappears, one turn at a time. She imagines her own leg bound with wire. She doesn't want to copycat, but you do have to keep up with trends. Maybe she'll do them both when the time comes.

ORIGINALLY APPEARED IN *PURE SLUSH*

54

Bones of the Founders

It was a dead city, street after street of brick buildings, windows boarded over, the tear tracks from their block letter names eroded to near invisibility. *Stritmeyers, J.C. Ward & Co., Good Humor.* A hot dog shop boasted a few cars parked outside. These were late model vehicles, well maintained. There was money somewhere in this burgh.

The traffic light turned red. Tom eased to a stop. A lemon-yellow Volkswagen Beetle puttered through the intersection. He played some options through his head. Giant Eagle had signed on to anchor one end of his shopping center, but he was torn between Nordstrom and Target for the other. Computer projections suggested they go high end. The WalMart three miles out of town was already pulling the low-end demographics. But he had a hunch. Something about this bricked-in downtown whispered Target to him, not Nordstrom.

A tap at his passenger window. Startled, he glanced over. A young woman was standing impatiently. Her straight blond hair reminded him of his youngest daughter's, but her face was more round, her lips fuller. She motioned him to open the window.

Tom buzzed the window down an inch. Her fingers immediately curled through the opening. Her eyes were blue sky under sunshine. Striking. You wanted to trust eyes like that.

"Let me in, okay?" Her teeth were as straight as her hair, as bright as her eyes. He hadn't expected this particular demographic in the rundown neighborhood.

"Why?" he said. Cold air leaked in. He took his foot off the brake. The car drifted forward. She drifted with it. "You don't even know me."

"But I do," she said. "You're T.S. Zealous, the shopping mall king."

Did she have a gun? His first impulse was to hit the accelerator, but something held him back. He told himself he didn't want to rip the girl's fingers off. He told himself it was market research. Below his thoughts, he knew better. There was something between them, an energy, a spitting hydraulic of... not lust. Affection?

"I have to talk to you," she said.

He unlocked the passenger door and watched her get in. She wore black pants, a bright blue shirt under a nondescript jacket. That reminded him of the chill outside. He flipped the passenger seat heater to *Warm*.

She nodded toward the windshield. "Light's green, Mr. Zealous."

"Tom," he said automatically.

"Green light, Tom."

I hope so. He pressed the accelerator. His back compressed the contoured seat. Acceleration and exhilaration had always been closely linked for him. He glanced over, sensing the firmness of the girl's body, the rabid youth of her emotions. He wanted to place his hand on her pant leg, squeeze. *Feel.*

"So," he said. "How do you know me?" In profile, she had a strong nose, the tip rounded.

"Your license plate," she said.

Tom nodded. *TZMALLZ 134* was pretty distinctive, but most people wouldn't know its meaning. One-hundred-thirty-four malls designed and constructed. *Soon to be 135.* He would need new plates.

"Are you an architectural student?" he said. There was a university branch near the city center.

"I was an artist." She gazed ahead.

"What are you now?" Tom said.

She laughed lightly. "Cindy."

"That's a pretty name," he said. "For a pretty girl." He wanted to call the words back. You didn't call girls pretty anymore, not since the 70's. Not since his first wife.

"Are you going to the Herald property?" she said.

"I was, yes." Tom negotiated a corner. "I have time for a coffee though."

"That's okay," Cindy said. "It's the Herald place I need to talk to you about."

Tom's mood shifted to wary. "What about it?"

"You purchased the property, right? You mean to turn it into a shopping mall."

"It's what I do," Tom said. "Let me guess. You're worried about cultural heritage. I assure you we'll do our best—"

"I'm concerned about the building."

"Oh." Now he did let his hand fall onto her thigh. Maybe he'd been wrong about their connection. If she was just another protestor he would drop her off at the next corner and be done with it. No harm in copping a feel first.

She did not seem to notice. He squeezed, feeling the thrill of taboo. Her body was nicely toned, the flesh delicious in the cup of his palm.

"What concerns you about the building?" he said.

"You have to keep it intact."

Tom moved his hand higher. Much more and they'd be breaking laws. Still, she didn't react. Sighing, he pulled his fingers back to the wheel.

57

"It's structurally unsound," he said. "We plan to use some of the bricks in the façade, however. It will be tasteful, you'll see."

"Keep the building," she said.

"Why?"

"It's the heart. Destroy it and you destroy the city."

Tom lifted his foot off the accelerator. The car slowed. "The project's been approved by the planning commission," he said. "It's a done deal."

"I have another idea for you to consider," Cindy said. She reached over and touched the back of his hand. Tom felt hot and cold in the same instant.

★★★

They stood outside a wrought iron gate. One side leaned from its broken hinges, the other rusted in place. There was barely enough room to squeeze through. A sign arced above. *Herald Estates.*

"Come with me," Cindy said. Tom still felt the imprint of her fingers on his hand. He frowned. Where was the car? Had he locked it? He did so much driving that he often lost track of time, but this felt different.

She led him across weed-infested asphalt. Once, this building must have been an impressive structure. Now it was a pile of bricks fighting a mostly losing battle with gravity. An architectural concept diagram depicting a cutaway of the building had been spray-painted onto a wall. The design showed a circular atrium bounded by walls honeycombed with rectangular recesses. Tom scratched his chin. *Am I dreaming?*

"It's lit by skylight," Cindy said. "You'll have to take out the upper floors."

"They've mostly taken themselves out," Tom said. He looked closer. "What are these openings? Ovens?"

58

"Crypts," Cindy said.

"I don't understand."

"We used to make steel here," Cindy said.

"I know that," Tom said. "It's time to move on. My mall will energize the city, Cindy, draw business downtown again, encourage IT employers, Health Care, maybe Green Energy."

"No," Cindy said. "It will kill us completely." She touched Tom's hand. An electric thrill ran through him. In a flash he knew her vision, crypts filled with bones from surrounding cemeteries, layer upon layer of foundry workers and craftsmen.

"The bones of the founders," she said. "They will reanimate the city."

"I don't know," Tom said. It made no sense, yet he could not deny the power of her idea. Tourists would come from around the world to see such a display.

"You do," she said. She leaned toward him. He closed his eyes, felt her lips on his. It was like being sucked through a vortex into some new life. He was inside her, she was inside him.

And then it was over. There was no spray-painted mural, no girl advocating her vision, only him standing alone in the shadow of a crumbling building. He glanced around, feeling embarrassed. He looked again at the brick wall. Did this building want to become a Nordstrum or a Target? That was the question he *should* be asking.

A cold gust rifled him. He pulled his arms tight. He hadn't even bothered to put on his jacket. Leaves danced along the ground. A black and white photograph dammed against his shoe. He bent and picked it up.

Cindy's face gazed from the scratched surface, light hair, full lips neutral. He gazed at the back of his hand where she had touched, where he had *imagined* her touching him. Whatever happened—Stroke? Walking Amnesia?—had left a powerful aftertaste.

A tingling sensation washed through him as he imagined these old bricks re-chinked, broken stones replaced with true facsimiles. It would be much more expensive, but what was the purpose of amassing a fortune if not to further passion? He smiled. Time to think outside the box store, T.S. Zealous. He might even go back to using his real name.

He placed the photograph into his shirt pocket, patted it once, and went to find his car.

ORIGINALLY APPEARED IN *LITERARY ORPHANS*

Office Rapport

We were in my office, that square of space set aside for indulgences, a desk crenelated with bright-lie photos of kids and wife, a wheeled chair, file cabinets, a drawer with paperclips, an oblong ashtray of jelly beans.

"You're blowing this out of proportion," Janice said. She laid her iPhone on the desk. The screen showed a graph with primary-colored lines that resembled a mountain range. Billings on the y-axis, month on the x. I leaned forward, careful not to kick the bundle wedged beneath the desk. A shudder scuttled through. I didn't want to think about who it was, why it was there. I'd been holed up all morning waiting for Management's shoe to drop.

I focused on the phone. "Is this supposed to reassure me?"

"Yes," she said. "It's not so terrible, Matt, it really isn't. Yes, you lost a potential client, but you'll bounce back. Remember last time?"

I nodded meekly and felt my face drain. "They said if it happened again I'd be sacked." There had been blood on the floor, blood-splattered walls. It had taken Janitorial a week to tame the smell.

"It's been four years," Janice said. "People forget. Raley's moved on, Jenkins is on vacation, your numbers are better than ever. It will be fine, trust me."

"Mondays are bad," I said. "I told Sarah—"

"I know," Janice said. "Sarah should never have let her past the waiting lounge." She reached across the desk for my hand. Her grip was firm. I longed for her certainty, a steady passion that could infuse a life without overwhelming it.

"Mondays are bad..." My voice trailed off, even as echoes of the weekend invaded my ears. Kids screaming, glass shattering, Beth's face slicked with tears and snot. *If you were a real man, you'd discipline them.*

"There's a meeting in twenty minutes," Janice said. She retrieved the iPhone and ticked through a few screens. "The O'Reilly merger. You're on due diligence for that, right?"

"Yeah." I sighed. O'Reilly was a douche, but I hadn't found anything solid to suggest he misled us. I glanced into the trough of shadow beyond my knees. "What about...?

"I'll speak to Juan," Janice said. "Don't worry, she'll be gone before you get back." She smiled. "I know how it is, Matt. Balancing family and work is a bitch."

"Thanks," I said, and now I did kick the body. For an instant it felt as if hands closed around my ankle, but, of course, that was impossible. I extracted my leg and pulled a letter opener free of the lump of flesh. The blade was bent.

"Requisition a new one," Janice said. "And stop by the Men's Room, okay? Wash your hands, brush your hair. You want to look presentable, right?"

"Yeah." I stood. The dead woman's eyes flashed in the flood of new light. I imagined Beth's wide eyes, the vein pulsing on her forehead. *Monday,* I thought. This was going to be a long week.

ORIGINALLY APPEARED IN PURE SLUSH

I Sold You a Mattress

To: {redacted}

From: m4w

Subject: Your intoxicating presence

I sold you a mattress set last night. You were with your daughters and your father. I loved you the moment I saw those milk chocolate cheeks. You smiled and the wide-openness of your gaze drew me out of my funk. Your daughters were cute too. I have a son about your oldest's age. I'm divorced. My wife has custody, but I'll have him this weekend.

I wanted to ask you out, but with your father there it was too awkward. He won't always be around, right? Do you live with him or something? Did your husband abandon you and the girls? Is that it? Did he die in Afghanistan? I'm sorry for your loss. I'll never leave you. I'll never die.

You said you would bring me a gift card today. For my service, my missing hand. I lost it in Iraq, not Afghanistan. I never knew your husband, if that's your angle. No, no, no, you don't have an angle, that's just me being paranoid, like when I reported those locals putting something in our food. Spices, the corporal said. Do you think he was lying? You know how they are. I ate the stew. It tasted funny. Everything tasted funny after that, like blow-torched sand, like liberty.

I hope you come tomorrow. I hope you bring that card. I'll spend it on coffee for you and your daughters. I can see the cream spinning down into that darkness, down and down until there's no difference.

Yours,

m4

★★★

To: m4w

From: {redacted}

Subject: Re: Your Intoxicating Presence

Dear Michael,

How did you get this email address? I'm not mad at you, but this could represent a serious security breech.

I do remember you. You have beautiful eyes, a beautiful soft voice. I can only imagine what you must have been like before the war. I'm sorry if that's cruel. It's just that I hold such resentment on this issue. If we never sent another young man into that godless place, I would be happy.

But it is what it is, and we must live the life we have to its fullest potential. I sense that you were having a difficult day and that you have perhaps attached an emotional significance to me that I do not deserve. I was there with my family, Michael. That was not my father, but my husband, whom I love very much. You may have noticed those other men keeping their distance. They accompany us everywhere. They carry guns. You do not want their attention, Michael, which is why I ask you never to contact me at this email, except to tell me how you came by the address in the first place.

I will see that you receive the gift card I promised. Spend it on your son. I'm sure he loves you very much.

Your friend,

Michelle

★★★

To: {redacted}

From: m4w

Subject: Re: Re: Your intoxicating presence

Ah, sweet Michelle, thank you for your reply. Sometimes I think that no one hears when I speak, including God, especially god. Sometimes I think I'm alone in the world and love is a dream.

A man in sunglasses gave me the gift card this morning. His smile was like a sardine's on thin-crust pizza. He said nothing, but he wanted to tackle me to the ground, wrap my arm into the small of my back and make me squeal. I think he loves you too, Michelle, and who can blame him?

Without you, the card is meaningless. I'll use it for a bookmark. As for how I obtained your email, don't you remember? You wrote it on my hand. I whispered in your ear and you wrote it in your lovely script. Your hair smelled like the ocean, so fresh. I wanted to run my fingers through your hair, but your father was there. Will he always be there? Can't we do something about that?

Yours,

m4

Ah, hell, Michael is my name (you have me)

★★✫

To: m4w

From: {redacted}

Subject: Re: Re: Re: Your Intoxicating Presence

Michael,

I did no such thing. How did you get this email? This is important.

And that was NOT my father, but the President of the United States. YOUR president, Michael. Please respect that in any future correspondence.

Michelle

★★★

To: {redacted}

From: m4w

Subject: Re: Re: Re: Re: Your intoxicating presence

I've made you mad. I'm so sorry, Michelle. It's the war. Iraq. I can't keep the rage out of me, it's like a wind blowing hot against my face, the smell of oil stinging my sinus cavities. We all have holes, Michelle, even you.

You did write on my hand. I put it under my pillow. I'll never wear it again. It's the altar I worship each morning, and the prayer I whisper every night.

We are meant to be. Are you beginning to understand?

Yours forever,

Michael

★★★

To: m4w

From: {redacted}

Subject: Re: Re: Re: Re: Re: Your Intoxicating Presence

My husband saw your emails, Michael. I assume his Chief of Security brought them to his attention, but I don't know for sure. It's not like him to snoop, but he's been acting strange lately. I

66

think he noticed how I looked at you in the furniture store. Maybe he saw... that other thing. I still don't remember writing on your hand, but you clearly have my email address and it came from SOMEWHERE. I think the stress of these last seven years have gotten to us both. I only hope the girls will be okay.

They'll be coming for you now, Michael. Don't fight them. Don't resist. I'll make sure you get the very best help available. This is not the end, but a new beginning.

M

★★★

To: {redacted}

From: m4w

Subject: Re: Re: Re: Re: Re: Your intoxicating presence

They're not coming, Michelle. Don't you understand? Those men in your story weren't there to protect you, but me. They watch over me. They'll watch over you too, and the girls, if you'll let them. Leave the rest of it behind. Don't tell your father.

Yes, a new beginning. Come to me, Michelle. Will you do that? Will you let the rest go, and come to me? I owe you a coffee ☺

Always,

Michael

★★★

To: m4w

From: {redacted}

Subject: Yes

ORIGINALLY APPEARED IN *ODDBALL*

Johnny Rotting

Explosion sculpts the air. Onstage, Johnny Rotting stops his gritty vocal. The building shakes with aftershock. Granular dust rains down.

"What the fuck!" someone shouts.

Johnny turns his deadpan stare onto the audience. "You don't speak, understand? I'm not here for you. You're here for me."

Three girls jump up and down, revealing the depth of their respective cleavages. "Keep playing, Johnny! We love you."

Johnny sneers. "I'm no one's pussy, you can't put me in your lap." He swings the guitar, the strap sliding across his bone-thin shoulder. Another explosion sounds.

"They're bombing the city," someone yells. The crowd takes on a nervous-excited vibe.

"Listen up," Johnny says. "Do not befriend the how-it-is. Get rid of it, take it down."

"Down with the fascist screed," the crowd chants. "Down with corporation greed."

Johnny cradles the microphone to his mouth. "Shout for me," he says, "and I'll destroy it all."

"John-ny! John-ny! John-ny!"

He pushes a violent chord onto the strings. "In case of fire," he says, "do not occupy the center, friends, move to the right or to the left." He cues the drummer. The audience goes wild.

Johnny sings:

"It's no use being nice.

No use in that at all.

You've got to do it hard and fast

You've gotta do it now.

Don't wait around for expertise.

Don't trash your self-respect.

It's the end game, the same game,

Time to choose your Pow."

In a bathroom across the street, a fat man strains to push urine past his swollen prostate. *God, let the building crumble,* he prays. *Let the whole world fall apart, but please help me finish peeing first.*

The floor shakes. His stream dribbles onto the toe of his shoe. *Shit.* The Stock Market has crashed. Looting is the new Retail. All he had left was dignity and now he's lost that.

Sounds of structure crumpling. Ceiling tiles go *splat*. Lights flicker off, leaving him alone and dark.

Words drift on the new equilibrium.

"It's no use blaming them.

No use in that at all.

You've got to pull your bootstraps up

You gotta make a buck.

Don't wait around for sympathy.

Don't bloat your self-esteem.

It's the end game, the same game,

Time to take that luck."

The whop-whop-chop of police copters coming in. A tear slides down the fat man's cheek. He tucks and zips and turns.

Cement pelts the crowd. Death everywhere. Commotion. Blood.

Even as the stage collapses, Johnny plays. Even as drums rattle incoherently and his microphone goes mute, his fingers form a chord. Unamplified, his voice goes into the round.

"There's no great trick to dying, friends.

Anyone can make a mound.

Even the purest cause

Creates an empty sound."

Summer

The slurp and grumble of rubber rolling over hot asphalt, a clattering grind as a hanger gives way and a section of rusted tailpipe drops down to taste the grayish grain. Laminar flow of sparks. It should put me in mind of the fireworks next week, the muffled boom and hiss, the intermittent squeals of color as the sky becomes a playground, movie screen, the only thing that matters. But I'm thinking of him, the old man by the men's shelter earlier today.

"Nice ladder," he says. "I designed that ladder," he says. "Did you know?" And of course, I don't, as his pale blue eyes water with expectation, as his hound-dog cheeks pull in with every rasping breath. He smells of body odor and something else. Fish guts? I don't know; it's not pleasant.

"You can do anything with that ladder," he says, and there's a hint of pride in his voice even has his trembling hand extends. I watch his palm, but it's only a handshake he wants, not money. There's a moment between us where neither of us is damaged and both of us are whole.

"I designed that ladder," he says, and I want to ask him when, where. I want to imagine him in a lab coat and goggles. Concentrating on something beyond another day.

I don't.

I don't imagine, don't ask, don't open myself to his attempted conversation. I'm afraid of the answers he will give, afraid of where interaction might lead. I think of the coins in my pocket, the credit cards in my wallet. I think that we'll both be dead in twenty years and none of it will matter.

"You can do anything with that ladder," he says.

71

You can do anything with anything, I think, *if you try*. I don't know if I believe it, but it's very American.

He frowns, blinks, swallows. I glance over my shoulder at the aluminum ladder leaning from my truck's bed. It's one of those devices you can configure into multiple shapes depending on the job.

He's waiting for me. Sadness hangs between us, a gathering storm. I think of the cool that rain will bring, an honest cleansing, renewal. It's been so hot. And then I think of how different it must be to have to live in the elements and endure a downpour. How the sun can be a blessing too.

I force myself to hold his gaze. "It really is a clever design." My throat catches. I feel tears welling up behind my eyes, and I don't even know why.

"Thank you," he says, and his lips form a half-smile. "Have a blessed day."

I reach for my wallet, but he's already shuffling down the sidewalk. I watch him stop at a store window, gather himself, straighten his spine, arms reaching high and higher toward the impossible sky.

ORIGINALLY APPEARED IN PURE SLUSH

Backlash

I press my skirt to my thighs and start a knock-kneed descent down the subway stairs. I should not have worn high heels, but I want to make a good impression on the first day of my first job out of college. This is an opportunity to be taken seriously.

I barely get through the turnstiles before it starts. "Hey, chicka, those are some nice legs you got. I bet they look good wrapped around my neck." He's standing by a bench along the tiled wall, a short, burly guy maybe 30, with an eight o'clock shadow. "Come on, chicka, throw me a little sugar, huh? Shake that money-maker."

I blow out a breath.

"Chicka, chicka, come to Daddy." He gives me a coy smile and slowly unzips his canvas jacket until the logo on his t-shirt is fully revealed. #DoMeToo. He pulls an iPhone from his pocket.

Damn. He's one of them.

Of course, I go to him. I can't afford to be dinged on social media and I haven't met a man here yet who can walk me to and from the office.

He lays me along the bench and proceeds to rape — or as it's called now — sample me. It's fast, relatively painless.

It happens again before I reach the boarding platform. This time the guy is well-kempt and wears a business suit that probably cost more than last semester's tuition. He flashes a business card with the #DoMeToo meme and we go into a bathroom stall.

He lifts my skirt an inch at a time. He's rougher than the first guy. It takes longer to complete the act, to the point that I worry I will miss the train. Then it's done, and I'm on my way again.

I think of semen mingling inside me, gooey and warm. In a sense I have become a vehicle for acquaintance. I have united two men from opposite ends of the economic spectrum. I should be proud, I guess, but the best I can muster is a tired acceptance. My role in this world appears to be less distinct from college than I had hoped.

Eventually, the train arrives at my stop. I emerge from the tunnel into a corridor of buildings that tower over me as my father once did. I don't have time to relish the scale of the moment with only minutes to spare, so I pinball along a sidewalk peppered with pedestrians until I find the address on the hire text. The doorman indicates his crotch. Five minutes later I'm in the elevator, the sour taste of him on my tongue. Tomorrow I must remember breath mints.

The elevator dings. The doors slide open. I hurry down a carpeted hall to a lobby lined with green plants. I pause to gather myself, straighten my skirt. Thank God that's over. Thank God I'm here.

A blonde sits at the reception desk gazing at a flatscreen. Her smeared lipstick tells me mine was not the doorman's first blowjob.

"I'm supposed to start today," I tell her.

She looks up without seeing. "Name?"

"Julia Stein."

Her attention returns to the screen, fingers poised above a keyboard. "Position?" She chuckles. "I guess that's up to them, huh?" She types. Her eyebrow arches. She acknowledges me for the first time. She's older than I thought. Silver roots mark the trough in her parted hair, crinkles show at the edges of her eyes.

"Looks like you've already had your orientation," she says. "Expect more of the same around here."

I shiver, recalling the feel of the concrete on my knees as people strode past. "I'm just trying to get by."

The blonde nods. "We all say that at some point." She sighs. "You weren't in the movement. You didn't feel that hope."

"What movement? What hope?"

The blonde shrugs. "Doesn't matter. Today's my last day." She glances at the screen and shrugs. "You're up next, kiddo."

A New Age

They sprayed us with inky demon shapes. We knelt, passive in the present, impassioned in the hidden time. And we were legion, us women of the world. We had been plotting the downfall of the Old Boys and on some level they understood. As willfully dense and sex-driven as they had become, they knew they were threatened.

Hisssssssssssssssssss... They pushed valves until their fingers bled, until spent cans clattered like shell casings, and still the tarry stuff flowed over us. Our hair ran black. We could barely breathe.

Cans ran dry and they used clubs, those phallic extensions of male authority. Skulls cracked, shoulders shattered.

Our line did not.

The last baton gave way, leaving them with mere fists and mouths. But that was nothing new. It could not last forever. Voices wear down and even knuckles have a limit.

When this ended, we stood as one, turned to each other, mended our bones, wiped our faces, combed our hair, scraped our bodies clean. Cans crunched beneath our feet.

Exhausted men knelt, heads bowed like flowers following the sun. Their guilt was palpable, a stench more vivid than the tar. We touched them, and they trembled. We lifted them up. They cried. We could have done anything to them in that moment.

What we did was kiss them, lick the salt from their faces, and murmur into their ears, "We forgive you."

A new Age had begun.

The Promised Land

"Welcome to this world," the Father of All Creation told his children. He set them adrift, gave each a paddle board and an oar tall enough to find substance beneath the waves. "There is your promised land," he said, pointing to far-off mountains perched along the horizon. "All you must do is paddle until you reach it."

And so, the children paddled. They paddled day and night, night and day through the troughs and swells of their lives, until their bodies were hard, and their minds closed to anything but their goal. Weeks became months, and though the horizon resolved into snow-crusted mountains, it seemed no closer.

"We'll never make it," a boy said. He was one of the strongest of them, tall and lean with curling golden hair.

"We won't if we don't keep going," another boy said. He slapped a wave with his oar for emphasis.

"No, he's right," a girl said. Her skin was dark, hair darker yet. "We're getting nowhere." She cast her paddle onto the water. A gasp sounded as it see-sawed down beyond anyone's reach.

Splash! A second paddle sank. The golden boy dropped onto his chest and swam to the girl. They touched, kissed.

"Ignore them!" the other boy shouted. "We're almost there." He resumed. Others followed, some reluctant, some with vigor.

Months became years. Bodies changed into adulthood. Still they paddled. The mountains seemed as distant as ever.

"I'm so hungry!" a woman shouted. She straddled her board.

"You can't stop now," the man who had become their leader said.

The woman sobbed. The paddle fell from her trembling hands, struck the board, and cantilevered down. She thrust her hand into the sea and her fist returned holding a small tuna.

"Ignore her," the leader said. "She made her choice." They left her gnawing contentedly on the fish.

Years became decades, and still the mountains seemed no closer.

"Is there another way?" a man said. He stroked his leathery face.

"There is only *the* way," the leader said. The now-familiar plop of an oar sounded, followed by a heavier splash. The man had jumped from his board and was skiing along the surface grasping a dolphin's fin. Several others followed his example.

"Be strong," the leader shouted. "We have but a short way to go."

As their journey continued, others faltered. Each time the leader commanded the rest to paddle on.

And then one day the leader glanced back only to discover that he was alone on the water. A sadness came over him such as he had never allowed. Tears burned his eyes. He lifted the oar and stared at his knob-knuckled hands, fingers curled so tightly around the wood that they may as well be a part of it.

"Promised land," he sighed. He was no closer than he had ever been. *Splash.* The oar dipped, stroked, emerged. Soon he was paddling again. Paddling. Paddling. What else could he do?

The Village Burning

The village is on fire again. Every Friday the village burns and every Saturday we rebuild it with time stolen from the end of our lives. When we were young it didn't matter so much. We loved the nightlife, the nakedness, the spirit-drugs that fueled our Fridays. We were happy to trade friction for fiction, which, of course, was what the future was. The only reality was the moment we were in.

Now that we are middle-aged it's not so fun watching the town burn and burn and burn, our lives consumed from the far end forward like the wick of a blood-scented candle. How do you stop something that has become engrained in culture? How do you put aside your childish things?

Religion is not the answer. No matter how many *Thou Shall Not Burns!* are shouted down the aisle, the church is ash by Friday midnight. We can't help ourselves it seems. For each of our sins there is a Father to forgive us.

We tried locking each other up, but someone had to hold the key. When the Friday itch arrived, it didn't matter how many were inside and how many without, there was no stopping the flame. Buildings charred to ash, iron bars melted in our hands. Time to rebuild again.

If only we had understood when we were young. If only we had guarded chastity, drank lemon water instead of rum, and sat quietly in our homes, there would have been no burning or rebuilding, just a steady, quiet flow.

We might have lived forever.

We Dissolve

One of these days, we will wake to explosion and poison gas, Sarin perhaps. We have to know that entropy demands this. We just hope to get enough life in before the end.

Audrey and I live in the forest now. Even from here, we see it happening. Politics settle across the world like radiation fallout, economic classes separate. Even a skim of oil is enough to deprive a lake of oxygen. We do not speak of this, but we feel it. We make love every night. In the morning we weep.

The brain is the first organ to go. Reason. Rationality. Altruism. Jesus becomes a brown-skinned boy holding a trout half as large as him, and his foot is on the water, and the water has become bedrock. And we, the common ones, the ones who matter, argue over which to worship, the boy or the fish, the miracle of water turned solid, or the reality of brown skin on our savior. We become Sumo wrestlers throwing salt, throwing pride, and the fat that forms us droops about our hips, our knees, touches the ground. As we drip away, we rail against those who outlast us. "Jesus boy," we pray, "Please destroy our enemies, take them deep into the Earth's fire and make them suffer." It's inevitable, this breaking apart, this falling apart, this sagging away of what was mighty.

I creep to the forest's edge and look out over fallow fields awaiting Winter. Breath condenses from my lungs. In the distance, factories with rusted-sheet sides belch smoke into the crystal sky.

Industry's puffing breath, one small slide down entropy's decline. So long as that stream continues, Audrey and I will live another day, and that is what matters.

A twig snaps. I turn. Audrey has followed me. So beautiful, that shocking orange nest of hair, high cheekbones full lips, the way her eyes light when they recognize. I feel an upswell. What was lost becomes real, the certainty of my worldview, the unbreakable armor of my love, the knowledge that reality begins and ends with my life. Brown Jesus' fish was meant for me.

The factory belches, burps, and goes still. A bubble releases from the sponge. I blink, and I see clearly again. Audrey's hair is a tangled mess, her skin covered in sores fresh and scabbed. As is mine, as mine will always and ever be until the end. Until now.

She moves beside me. Supple fingers wind through my stubby ones. I want to embrace her, cover her, insulate. *Too late.* My nose runs, my chest pulls in. I cannot breathe.

Dissolving, I turn to Audrey. Her eyes are watching too.

ORIGINALLY APPEARED IN *GONE LAWN*

That Beautiful World

In the beautiful world we knew as children there was no brimstone, only introspection, a chance to gather ourselves from the glorious treachery of a day lived full. We sank onto knees scuffed and scraped from play and asked for love in a voice that moved inside us like fabric turning inside out. We glimpsed the quilting of our lives in those slow minutes, the way things work, the benevolence of a God only imaginary before. He was real. We were matchsticks and He the flame that lit us.

When it was over, we would stand and, for a few seconds more, silence cloaked us. Then, with the sharp persistence of the inevitable, noise returned, the noise of the city, the noise of our troublesome flesh.

Love pounded by ticking seconds cannot endure. Glittering dust settles into shadow and we are left to deal with ourselves. Your heaven is not my heaven and my heaven is not yours.

Predatory shadow, sharp-toothed mantra gnawing until only blood is real and violence our means of communication.

Do you wonder what might have changed had we not turned from each other? Imagine God touching your face—warm as the sun—me falling to my knees beside you. And as the dirt sprinkles from my fist, imagine it clinging to our skin until we are once again cocooned in that beautiful world.

ORIGINALLY APPEARED IN *APOCRYPHA AND ABSTRACTIONS*

If you enjoyed this book, please check out *Glass Animals* from Pure Slush Books.

Praise for *Glass Animals*:

He seamlessly weaves a crazy-quilt of characters who - despite being a little lost and befuddled by the world - have moments of chandelier insight into their own human hearts. Reminiscent of Raymond Carver's *Little Things* and Kim Chinquee's *Oh Baby*, *Glass Animals* is a work of sparkling vision and compressed and surprising language - all put to work to reveal a world where everything's at stake. - **Lori Jakiela**, author of *Miss New York Has Everything*

Ramey takes on the richness of his characters' emotional and physical torment and delivers something morbidly fascinating and keen. - **Kristine Ong Muslim**, author of *We Bury the Landscape*

Stephen V. Ramey captivates and mesmerizes his readers, taking us by the hand into the hidden worlds of people not unknown to us. His instincts are visceral, perceived, radiating a power and compassion that guides us inside each of his characters. Ramey's collection explores the human condition. Ramey is the real thing. - **Meg Tuite**, author of *Domestic Apparition*

Glass Animals is one of those rare short story collections where every story is great. Stephen V Ramey takes the reader on wild adventures, with stories that are hilarious, poignant, and powerful. Ramey is a master of the short craft, and he pulls it off whether the story is a half-page or ten pages. Although the stories aren't strongly connected to each other, Ramey's pacing and prose makes this book addictive. – **TowerOPower** (Amazon Review).